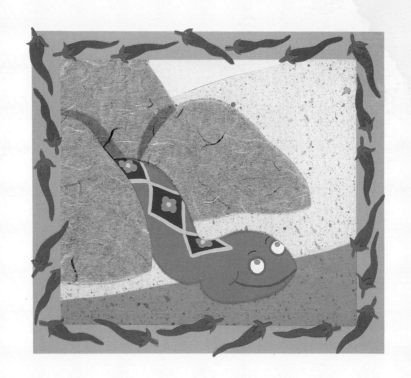

*For my mother, with love – L. M.*

*For Lenny, Lucy and Olivia in Australia
and Leonie in New York, with love – Mira*

Design: Marilyn Musgrave and Armagh Cassil
    SOMAR Graphics
Typesetting: Berna Alvarado-Rodriguez
    Metro Type
Photography: Joe Sambery

Printed in China through Marwin Productions

Children's Book Press is a nonprofit community publisher.

Library of Congress Cataloging-in-Publication Data

Ata, Te.
  Baby Rattlesnake / told by Te Ata; adapted by Lynn Moroney; illustrated by Mira Reisberg.
  Summary: Willful Baby Rattlesnake throws tantrums to get his rattle before he's ready, but he mis-
uses it and learns a lesson.

  1. Chickasaw Indians–Legends.  2. Rattlesnakes–Folklore.  3. Indians of North America–Southwest,
New–Legends.  {1. Chickasaw Indians–Legends.  2. Indians of North America–Southwest, New–
Legends.  3. Rattlesnakes–Folklore.}  I. Moroney, L.  II. Reisberg, Mira.  III. Title.
E99. C55A73  1989  398.24'52796'089973–dc20  89-9892  CIP  AC

# Baby Rattlesnake

TOLD BY TE ATA

ADAPTED BY LYNN MORONEY

ILLUSTRATED BY MIRA REISBERG

Children's Book Press
San Francisco, California

**O**ut in the place where the rattlesnakes lived, there was a little baby rattlesnake who cried all the time because he did not have a rattle.

**H**e said to his mother and father, "I don't know why I don't have a rattle. I'm made just like my brother and sister. How can I be a rattlesnake if I don't have a rattle?"

Mother and Father Rattlesnake said, "You are too young to have a rattle. When you get to be as old as your brother and sister, you will have a rattle, too."

But Baby Rattlesnake did not want to wait. So he just cried and cried. He shook his tail and when he couldn't hear a rattle sound, he cried even louder.

Mother and Father said, "Shhh! Shhh! Shhhhh!"

Brother and Sister said, "Shhh! Shhh! Shhhhh!"

But Baby Rattlesnake wouldn't stop crying. He kept the Rattlesnake People awake all night.

The next morning, the Rattlesnake People called a big council. They talked and they talked just like people do, but they couldn't decide how to make that little baby rattlesnake happy. He didn't want anything else but a rattle.

At last one of the elders said, "Go ahead, give him a rattle. He's too young and he'll get into trouble. But let him learn a lesson. I just want to get some sleep."

So they gave Baby Rattlesnake a rattle.

**B**aby Rattlesnake loved his rattle. He shook his tail and for the first time he heard, "Ch-Ch-Ch! Ch-Ch-Ch!" He was so excited!

He sang a rattle song, "Ch-Ch-Ch! Ch-Ch-Ch!"

He danced a rattle dance, "Ch-Ch-Ch! Ch-Ch-Ch!"

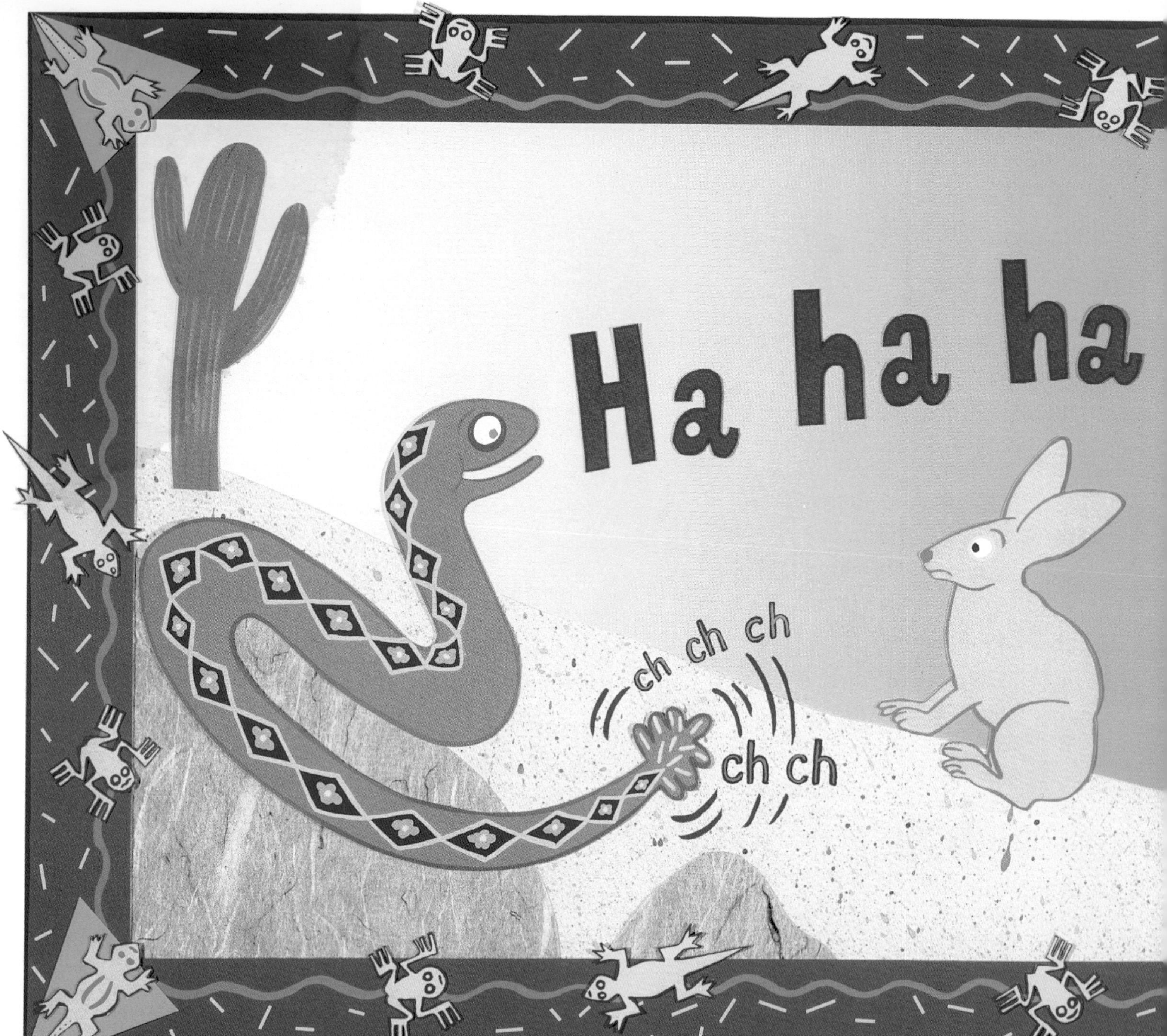
Ha ha ha
ch ch ch
ch ch

ha  ha

Soon Baby Rattlesnake learned to play tricks with his rattle. He hid in the rocks and when the small animals came by, he darted out rattling, "Ch-Ch-Ch!"  "Ch-Ch-Ch!"

He made Jack Rabbit jump.
He made Old Man Turtle jump.
He made Prairie Dog jump.

Each time Baby Rattlesnake laughed and laughed. He thought it was fun to scare the animal people.

other and Father warned Baby Rattlesnake, "You must not use your rattle in such a way."

Big Brother and Big Sister said, "You are not being careful with your rattle."

The Rattlesnake People told Baby Rattlesnake to stop acting so foolish with his rattle.

Baby Rattlesnake did not listen.

One day, Baby Rattlesnake said to his mother and father, "How will I know a chief's daughter when I see her?"

"Well, she's usually very beautiful and walks with her head held high," said Father.

"And she's very neat in her dress," added Mother.

"Why do you want to know?" asked Father.

"Because I want to scare her!" said Baby Rattlesnake. And he started right off down the path before his mother and father could warn him never to do a thing like that.

The little fellow reached the place where the Indians traveled. He curled himself up on a log and he started rattling. "Chh-Chh-Chh!" He was having a wonderful time.

All of a sudden he saw a beautiful maiden coming toward him from a long way off. She walked with her head held high, and she was very neat in her dress.

"Ah," thought Baby Rattlesnake. "She must be the chief's daughter."

**B**aby Rattlesnake hid in the rocks. He was excited. This was going to be his best trick.

He waited and waited. The chief's daughter came closer and closer. When she was in just the right spot, he darted out of the rocks.

"Ch-Ch-Ch-Ch-Ch!"

o!" cried the chief's daughter. She whirled around, stepping on Baby Rattlesnake's rattle and crushing it to pieces.

aby Rattlesnake looked at his beautiful rattle scattered all over the trail. He didn't know what to do.

He took off for home as fast as he could.

With great sobs, he told Mother and Father what had happened. They wiped his tears and gave him big rattlesnake hugs.

For the rest of that day, Baby Rattlesnake stayed safe and snug, close by his rattlesnake family.

# ABOUT BABY RATTLESNAKE

Internationally-acclaimed storyteller Te Ata, a Chickasaw Indian born 92 years ago in the Oklahoma Territory has been regaling audiences in the USA and Europe for more than 65 years. *Baby Rattlesnake*, a teaching tale about what happens when you get something before you're ready for it, is one of her best-loved tales.

Oklahoma storyteller Lynn Moroney, herself part Indian, had admired Te Ata for years and finally asked her permission to retell the story of *Baby Rattlesnake*. At first the answer was no, but when Te Ata came to a story-telling festival organized by Lynn and heard the younger woman tell her own stories, Te Ata was so impressed that she gave Lynn her blessing to tell this story and pass it on to others through the medium of a book.

Artist Mira Reisberg fell in love with the story of Baby Rattlesnake the moment she heard it. "I can identify with that loveable brat," she says, "and the best part is that he is forgiven with big rattlesnake hugs." Her medium for this book is cut paper and gouache paints. Mira was born in Australia and has lived in the Southwest United States, the setting of *Baby Rattlesnake*. She now lives in San Francisco where she recently illustrated *Uncle Nacho's Hat*, also published by Children's Book Press.

A special thanks goes to San Francisco Bay Area Storyteller Gay Ducey, who brought Lynn's original manuscript to Children's Book Press and then nurtured the project on its way to completion.

Thanks also to Glenn Hirsch, Helene Vosters, Annee Boulanger, Cynthia Lane, Maggie Crystal, and David Schecter for their inspired assistance.

Children's Book Press publishes global literature for children, featuring both traditional and contemporary stories from minority and new immigrant cultures in America today. Write us for a free catalog.